Nikhil Saikia

Invincible Publishers

First published in India in 2019

ISBN : 978-93-88333-82-5

Invincible Publishers

Registered Address: 201A, SAS Tower, Sector 38,
Gurgaon-122003

Printed at Thomson Press (India) LTD

This book is dedicated to my friends and family, who always choose to love me.

Acknowledgements

I would like to thank my family, friends and everyone else, who cared to read my stuff and provided feedback.

Big thanks to my friends for your constant support and encouragement, and for reading everything I sent you. I am lucky to have you all.

A big thanks also to my father, brother and cousins, for always standing with me.

And finally, I love you Maa.

Introduction

Hi, I am Aarush. I was not used to serious, complicated situations. I loved myself as a person. I loved everyone in my life and I respected the dynamics of the relationship they had with me. I always believed that God had a perfect plan for me. It helped me to maintain a smile on my face and not lose my temper easily. Everyone tackles their past in their own way, while carrying different emotions in their heart. Each one is filled with memories worth remembering or moments that they are unable to erase.

Time is the best teacher. During the good times, it teaches in such a manner that you feel like you are attending the best class in the world. But if you do not give your 100% in those classes, the situation may change. There are only two results which count: Pass or fail. Just like the binary numbers, 0 and 1. Either you score 0 or 1; there is no middle route. Most importantly, you can't jump to the next class until and unless you score 1 in the current one. You can move on with 0. But for that, you have to take another route. And it's difficult to decide whether to take that second route or try to score 1 once again. It becomes even more difficult if it seems like life is giving you the chance to change your score to 1. So the best class, where everything seemed perfect, might suddenly turn into the curse of your life. Even if you try to redo everything with 200% effort, it may not count. Now you are left with two options: Take another route, or try to score 1 and get back everything you let go of earlier.

Taking another route is always in your hands. Once you move on that alternate path, you have no idea what you are leaving behind. And challenging the life you know is once again not fully under your control. Here you can just give your best efforts. There is no guarantee of scoring that elusive 1. Again, you may score 0 or 1. Your efforts may not be accepted to score what you desire and in the process, may be rendered completely obsolete as well. Since you are up against life, you can't appeal against it anywhere. You can either accept your situation as your destiny or try to change your fate. Life is all about turning those 0s into 1s. One good class gives you a pleasant memory, worth cherishing for a lifetime and one bad class gives you that important learning experience.

Present Day

AARUSH:

It was a rainy March morning. I found myself sitting at the café by the Ambari bus stop. That day, I was jealous of the younger me; the person I was just a few years back. How I used to keep my smile brimming at all times, without any pretense.

"Will you say something? I came here directly from the airport. That too early in the morning at 5:30". It was Pari, almost shouting at me.

"Ok" I responded to her statement that pierced through the pleasant silence.

"What ok, Aarush?" she continued, "Ok is the third thing you have said after 'hi' and 'nice coffee'. Stupid!"

I smiled at her reaction. Actually, some part of me was sweating inside that fully air conditioned room. A part of me was struggling to cope with the situation at hand. I had been preparing for long, trying to act brave for this moment. And at last, when she arrived, the words just refused to come out of my mouth. Though Pari and I were classmates, I have bonded with her in the real sense only in the past six months.

"You know, I hate this smile of yours" Pari continued in her normal tone, "You always avoid so many things with that smile."

Though she looked calm, I could see the curiosity in her eyes. I didn't react to her accusations. I just pulled out my diary from my backpack and passed it on to her.

PARI:

I was just stepping out of my office when I had received Aarush's message. It read "what's the plan this weekend?"

I have always been amazed by Aarush's weird surprises. We were in the same batch in school, but over the years, we had lost touch. I was pursuing my degree at the same University of Tezpur where he did his MBA. It has been only six months since we had reconnected. And then one day, I bumped into my old friend at the metro station, just out of the blue. And in the past six months, I have discovered a new facet of his personality. A side I had not seen during our days at the University. Now, he is like an ocean full of mystery. He has a tendency of very cleverly concealing the kind of person he actually is. I had never heard him speak ill of others. I had always seen him smile. Sometimes I envied him. Maybe, I have started liking him. Maybe, he is the person I have been waiting for so long.

After reaching home, I texted him back "Nothing special. Just like any other weekend."

"You like stories? Check your email" I read the strange reply from Aarush. Sometimes he does not say exactly what he means. You need to infer from the limited information he provides and extrapolate it to make it meaningful. I have decided not to waste my time and energy on trying to decipher the meaning of his message before opening the email he sent.

To my surprise, the email had an attachment of a ticket from Delhi to Guwahati. I was shocked!

I dialed his number immediately, “What is this, Aarush?”

“Don’t tell me you are not excited?” Aarush spoke in his regular tone.

“But 5:30 in the morning?! Even the sun doesn’t rise so early”, I said, in a clearly irritated tone.

“Sorry, Pari! It was the cheapest ticket available”. I could tell it was an honest answer.

Honestly, I was excited. He has always been an inspiring person and for the last 3 months, after he shifted to Guwahati, we hadn’t met. I was eagerly waiting for the Saturday morning.

The Diary

AARUSH

I left for the shopping complex directly after my class. A lot of things were happening for the first time with me. I failed in the midterm. I had skipped football practice sessions and I had lost something important. It had become difficult for me to smile. I could not figure out the best way to fix things. I started arguing with my inner self. I thought he might have the answers I was searching for.

After finishing my cup of coffee, I got up with the intention to leave. This seemingly average day had not been good so far.

"Hello!" said someone. I turned to see if I knew who it was. It was Tia, my classmate. I replied in a low voice "Hi." I couldn't remember the last time we had a proper conversation. I turned back and started walking again.

"Are you ok?" the same voice was asking.

I replied, "Yes, I am".

At that moment, I was not in the right frame of mind to start a conversation. That too with a girl! I wanted to escape as soon as possible. The shy part of my personality always tries to maintain a safe distance from girls.

"Hey, would you like to join me for a cup of coffee?", she asked rather politely. "Would you like to have another one?"

I nodded and sat down on the platform. She pulled the chair and placed it diagonally so that we could both avoid eye contact. I didn't realize for how long we had remained seated like that. I sensed she wanted to say something, but I was not in a mood to listen. As soon as we finished our coffee, I said, "So see you."

"Can we talk for a while? I feel like you need some company "Tia said.

I was surprised by those words and confused at the same time. I could feel my heart beating, loudly. "Sorry, I really need to go now". The words came out automatically, as if I was not in control of my lips. "And thanks for the coffee."

I just wanted to get away from the situation. Maybe she was right. I needed to talk. I needed company. I didn't know how she felt. Was it clear from my behavior that I was trying to escape the situation? In truth, I actually was in no rush to go anywhere. I felt guilty. "Maybe I should apologize next time I meet her", I thought to myself.

TIA'S DIARY

I have never seen Aarush so gloomy before. Even though we are not best of friends, we still have been classmates for eight months now. His trademark smile was missing today. The warmth he carries with him always fills the class with positive vibes. There must be something wrong or he just hasn't overcome his loss. I can't even imagine a day without my mother. He needs help. His marks in the midterm exams clearly say that he is unable to concentrate. I don't know if he will ever have a heart-to-heart talk with me. However, I want to know his story.

AARUSH

The next day I was a bit nervous owing to the coffee incident at the shopping complex. I wanted to tell Tia that I was sorry for the way I behaved. During the tea break, I reached the lobby and said to her "I am sorry for yesterday. Please don't misunderstand me."

She smiled at my words, "Stupid, no need to be sorry."

For the first time, I actually noticed her. She was indeed beautiful. The black mole just on the right side of her nose is like the sprinkles on an ice cream. She offered me some biscuits and asked "So, can I expect coffee after class?"

I didn't say anything. I just smiled at her words. "Keep smiling. It suits you", Tia said. As we began to talk, Rishi, my roommate, joined us and ended our short one-to-one conversation.

When she came for coffee in the evening, I was with Rishi. "Welcome Queen," Rishi greeted her. Rishi was renowned for his flirtatious nature. He was quite popular among girls. Our personalities were poles apart but he was one of my best buddies.

"You will have coffee, right?" Rishi asked Tia.

"Yes, I mean maybe" Tia stammered, trying to reply to his stupid enquiry.

"Good, you both wait here and give me the key to your cycle", Rishi told Tia.

"Ok, but don't be late", Tia said.

Rishi and I exchanged a meaningful smile. Tia noticed but she was only concerned about her cycle.

"Don't worry. Its fifteen minutes walk from the engineering department to the girl's hostel," I assured her.

"So, we are friends finally?", Tia raised her palm for a high-five. I didn't show any excitement. I just smiled at her.

"Do you think friendship is a deal?", I asked. "A deal that is started suddenly by saying let's be friends or something like that?"

Tia looked confused and put her hand down saying, "I didn't mean anything like that". She was looking cute in those spectacles with the yellow frame.

"Hey, obviously we are friends. And I don't feel we need to announce it in front of an audience," I said.

"Yes, spot on" Tia continued. "By the way, I can help you in accountancy", this was a suggestion that came out of the blue.

I gave her a confused look. I couldn't understand the reason behind this nice gesture of hers. I knew she was good in accountancy. She was a graduateW in it.

I asked, "What do you mean?"

"Look Aarush, yesterday, I noticed that you were very upset after getting your marks. I can help you. And anyway, assignments are to be done in groups of two. We can be partners if you don't mind" she said. She further added, "and of course, if Rishi doesn't mind." I could sense something mischievous in her last words.

I said, "Ok let's see. I have got to go now. I am thinking of resuming football practice from today."

"How mean?! Wait till your roommate is back with my cycle", Tia threatened mischievously.

Then we sat there for some time, in silence. I don't know what she was thinking. But I felt that urge again. I wanted to escape. I was getting really uncomfortable again. My shy side was surfacing.

"If you want to sit like this, you are free to go", Tia said.

I resisted my basic urge. I quickly went to the grocery store and bought two chocolates, "Have a break, have a Kit Kat", I said and offered one to her.

"I love chocolates. But I don't like wafers", Tia said.

"Why should you be so choosy? Just enjoy whatever comes your way," I said, feeling a bit more in control.

"But I don't like to being diplomatic", Tia said.

I smiled at her and said "everything has something positive within. From today's "Kit Kat" incident, you can be sure that next time you will get a Cadbury."

She laughed at my answer. Meanwhile, Rishi was back and grinning from ear to ear with his customary smile.

"Ooh Kit Kat, I am loving it". With those words, he snatched half of my chocolate. Then, we bid farewell to one another.

AARUSH'S DIARY

I don't know why I feel good when I am with her. Till a few days ago, she was almost a stranger. But now, she is starting to take a special place in my list of friends. Initially, I was surprised by her proposal to be partners for accountancy, but it's a fair deal for me. I am in. I don't like baring myself to other people; or rather, I don't like to share the details of the person I actually am, with anyone else.

Her demanding nature is adorable. It's hard to evade her questions with just a smile. Although I feel vulnerable when I am with her, I still want to meet her. Maybe she is also hiding a lot within her. I am going to be her partner.

TIA'S DIARY

Aarush, the cool boy in our class, might be hiding a lot of things in his heart. He always tries to protect his innermost feelings with that perfect smile. Yes, he has the cutest smile I have ever seen. Yesterday I thought he was upset because of his low marks. But today, I am sure it's not about the marks. I want to know him. Everyone talks about his sense of humor, his presence of mind, his kindness and selflessness towards his friends. I want to be one of his friends. I hope he accepts my partnership proposal for the accountancy paper.

AARUSH: *The Football Match*

"Hey, Aarush! You have to play today! Be on the field sharp at 5:30 in the evening" Riyan told me. I was a bit surprised because I didn't play in any of the qualifying matches in the tournament and was not prepared to directly give my all the finals. Riyan, a research scholar, who was two years elder to me, was the captain of our hostel team.

I stared at Riyan for a while and muttered, "I haven't practiced".

"Yes, that's why I am calling you at 5:30 pm. You are always in good shape. Just come two hours before the match begins. The match is scheduled at 7:30 pm. And you are the best fullback we have", Riyan said before I could say anything.

"Ok, I will be there but you need to rethink this decisions to include me in the final 11", I reminded as I couldn't refuse.

"See you in the evening", said Riyan and left with a smile.

I was still confused. I noticed Tia was still looking at me. She was dying to say something.

"Hey, you play football", she exclaimed. I was struggling to understand whether it was a question or a statement. But Rishi made it easy. "Stupid, haven't you seen him in inter-department tournaments? My roomie is a hero", Rishi said. I looked at him and I could see that he was not surprised by Riyan's offer to me.

"Hey, hey!! I am not that good, ok! And I am still deciding whether to play or not!" I said.

"C'mon roommate, you have to play. I will bring the supporters", Rishi was excited by then. I, on the other hand, couldn't find any reason to be excited.

I reached the field, sharp at 5:30. Riyan came up to me and threw jersey no. 11 at me. "You are in the starting 11," he said. I started to jog with him but was still confused. This was the first time that I was so unprepared for a football match. Still, I started kicking the football. It's always fun to have the ball at my feet.

We played well. I played fine as well, but we lost it in the penalties.

"Hey, it seems you are a famous player", Tia told me after the match.

I smiled and said, "It's Rishi, stupid! I suspect he paid the girls to chant my name".

Tia laughed at my reply, "You are not that bad. You deserve to be famous", Tia said.

"Name some footballers across the world?", I asked her.

"Ronaldo, Messi...hmm... oh yes Aarush", she said with a smile.

"See, you know only two names. Almost every country plays this game. India's rank fluctuates between 140 to 160. Now see, to certify me as a famous football player, you have to know lakhs of players across the world". She seemed confused with my answer explaining why I cannot be considered a famous football player.

"But you are famous among football lovers on the campus", she said in an attempt to prove her point. She continued, "Especially among female supporters". I could sense something fishy in her words. But I was not bothered to probe further.

My phone rang. "Where are you? Come soon!" It was Rishi over the phone that ended our conversation once again. "Let's go", I said to Tia. I stood and prepared to leave the community hall by the playground. Walking around the campus has always been a pleasure. As it was late, I felt it was my duty to accompany Tia to her hostel on the other side of the field. Maybe she didn't expect me to do that. She got down from her cycle and we started walking. Though I tried to act confident, but a big part of me was scared. I was looking out for any familiar eyes which might be following me. I looked at Tia. She was enjoying the walk. It took almost 10 minutes to reach her hostel. We didn't speak a word on our way. "So, good night", Tia said.

"Yes, thank you", I was really nervous standing in front of the girls' hostel.

"Stupid, say good night", said Tia, mocking my situation. I bid her good night and hurried back to my room.

When I reached my wing in the hostel, I could only say “Oh my God!” It was a full on party. One of the security guards at the hostel had arranged for a harmonium and the guys at the hostel had started a musical night.

“Hey Aarush, come”, someone yelled from the crowd. I couldn’t identify the speaker. Rishi was almost sloshed by then. I have often faced such situations, so I knew what I should do. I stayed with them for some time and then got up to go back to my room.

“Rishi, are you coming?”, I asked Rishi.

“Yes bro, please help me”, Rishi requested. I took him to our room. He was unable to walk properly, but the blabbering never stopped. Though I couldn’t figure out what it was all about, I surmised that the party was arranged in honour of our loss at the football field, sort of a tragedy party. I laughed in my head. Rishi can turn any situation into an atmosphere fuelled by fun and enjoyment.

AARUSH:

Dhap dhap dhap...! I woke up before the clock ticks 9 in the morning with the sound of my door. Normally we don't celebrate or acknowledge the morning on Sundays except during some special occasions. I reluctantly opened the door. Avi rushed into the room. He was looking tensed.

"Hey, Rishi! Wake up!", Avi pulled Rishi's legs.

"What happened?" I asked Avi.

Avi was frantic, "We are finished. Someone complained about last night's party and now we have been summoned to the VC's office at 10:30".

"What? Can you please elaborate?", I was curious. If it was true then, it's a big issue.

"Nothing to elaborate on. Some guy from our hostel complained about last night's party. He probably mentioned some names. According to Riyan, Rishi and I are on the list", Avi alleged.

"Oh my god, who would do that?", I muttered.

"How do I know?", Avi said. "You get him ready, and do everything not to stint".

After that, Avi went out of the room. I got busy trying to restore the shape of my room and forced Rishi to wake up. Poor Rishi, he was still unaware of the storm coming towards him. Finally, I was successful in waking him up.

"Oh, my head!" Rishi was speaking to his own self.

"Forget about your headache. Brush and freshen up quickly", I said to him.

"Who came in the morning? It must be Avi. He always disturbs my morning sleep", Rishi went on.

"Hey, it's serious. Someone double-crossed you people. Now, five of you are summoned to the office around 10:30. I don't know who are the five, but according to Avi, yours and Avi's name is there on the list. You go and take a bath", I informed Rishi. I tried to explain the complex situation. Rishi was yet to leave his bed. I could see the tension on his face, rising from the uncertainty of the outcome. It was obvious that the situation was going to be tough. Now all we could do was wait. Through all this tension, Rishi was still trying to be his normal self.

TIA

The news spread like a forest fire. Our department became famous within the campus. The disciplinary committee almost broke the spirit of the evergreen twosome, Rishi and Avi, but even after several rounds of grilling, the punishment was yet to be announced.

"Hello, Rishi. Come to the cafeteria. My mom brought Biryani today. And tell Aarush and Avi too. They are not picking my call. Don't be late, ok?" My parents came to visit me in the morning. Last time, when they bought biryani, I shared it with girls. But now, this time around, it was booked for the boys.

"Ok, we are never late for a treat", Rishi said and cut the line.

I waited almost 30 minutes for them, but they never turned up. Finally, I could see the three walking towards me.

"You are so late. I have been waiting since 11, and now it's 11:40", I was irritated by their perpetual lack of respect for other people's time.

"It's hardly a 5-minute walk", I continued.

"We were coming by bike", Rishi said.

"Oh really? That is funny, "I said

"Yes, but that's not funny. We were three and now, Avi's bike is been ceased for tripling ", Aarush said with full empathy for Avi.

"Yes, Avi tried to convert his bike into a rickshaw", Rishi Joked

"Then what happened?", I was curious.

"What else? The bike is now in front of the administrative block, chained and padlocked", Aarush replied

I found it funny. It was not so funny in front of the disciplinary committee.

"So, today is the verdict day right?", I asked while serving them biryani in the plate.

"Yes. Let's hope for the best and prepare for the worst. We already fixed one rented house in front of the gate, in case we are rusticated from the hostel", Rishi said.

"Hmm. Let's see what happens. You will get back your bike soon, right?", I asked.

"Yes, Riyan's uncle is in humanities department. He said I will get it by evening", Avi said.

They finished with the food and left for their room. I too headed towards the room. I was unable to talk to them with a free mind. I was surprised they were still cracking jokes and smiling. This is going to be one of the tensest and important evenings of our group and obviously of their varsity life.

When I reached the shopping complex in the evening, I saw our group seating on the steps.

"Hi. Come have a seat", Aarush offered me his chair.

I thanked him and took my place. They were already deeply involved in the case. They were talking about possible situations. But none were sounding too good. One person said that the university's stand was that they did not consider them to be guilty. Instead, they looked at them as victims. We all agreed, of all the possibilities, this was the least likely one. We passed an hour or so waiting for Rishi and Avi.

Finally, they came with the verdict. They had rusticated from the hostel for one semester. Though we guessed something like that, we were still broken by the news.

AARUSH

Tia and I became very good friends by the third semester. Our partnership in the accountancy paper ended on a good note. I secured the required passing marks and it was satisfying. We still continued to study together. We loved to tackle some of the mind-boggling chapters in our own way. The days were breezing by just like it all started. And moreover, my roommate rejoined me.

"Hey, help me with this operations paper, please!", Tia said to me while we were returning from class.

"Why? Concentrate in the class", I said casually. I was a bit surprised by her silence. I had never seen her so silent. She always contradicts my stupid statements. She was distracted. She was not mentally present in the moment.

"Hey, what happened?", I said to break the silence.

"Nothing, I was just thinking", she said and paused for a moment. That moment stretched on for quite some time. I didn't ask her anything. I felt she had a lot of things stacked in her heart. But I was not sure whether I was the right person to know her story. I had never believed in rumours about the people close to me. Tia and I had developed a close bond by then and I wanted her to reveal any secrets she might have in her own sweet time. I did not want to dig around for further information.

"It's ok. Thinking is a good habit and sometimes it proves that you have brain", I tried to cut through the air of tension. She smiled at my poor joke.

"Are you free in the evening?", I asked her.

"I don't know. Why?", she enquired.

"Good then. You help me with the balance sheet for my summer project. I need it urgently. Let's meet at 7 p.m. in the cafeteria tomorrow", I told her

"But, my operations paper…", she said

"Ok…", I said and left for my room.

Rishi had developed a fever by the evening. But, that didn't stop him from going out on his routine outing to the shopping complex. I accompanied him for a cup of coffee. The ever excited Rishi was quite sober that day.

"Let's go to the room", Rishi said after finishing his coffee. I nodded. I took him to the hostel and headed for the cafeteria. Tia was already there. "Hey, good evening!", I wished her before taking my seat opposite to her. She smiled back at me, but that effervescent spark was lacking in her smile.

We had just started with the first problem when I saw Rishi's text, "Hey bro, where are you?", I didn't reply. But I got up and said to Tia, "Can we reschedule this for another day?"

"Ok, but what happened?", she said.

"Nothing serious. Rishi has a fever and he might need something", I said.

"But, what about your balance sheet? You have to give the presentation tomorrow", Tia reminded me.

"I will take care of it. Anyways after completing our course here, we won't remember how much we scored. We will only remember the memories we created, the bonds we developed", I smiled.

"How can you be so confident about your friends?", Tia asked.

"By that logic, I should doubt you too", I replied. "I will choose to go to a roadside dhaba in an auto with friends rather than driving a Ferrari alone".

"And what if your friends choose the other option?", Tia questioned.

"Then we will go to the dhaba in my friend's Ferrari", I replied with a smile.

"As if!", Tia muttered to herself.

"Why, wouldn't you give me a ride if you manage to buy a Ferrari one day?", I asked.

"Forget it. Let's go. Your friend, the potential Ferrari owner, is waiting for you", she mocked as we left for our respective hostels.

TIA'S DIARY

Aarush is a friend to cherish. Today, I wanted to spend some more time with him. His company gives me the warmth that I am missing most of the time. Here I am, trying to make my life perfect, whereas he is just living his life and thus making it perfect in his own way. I feel he knows I am in the midst of an emotional crisis. Maybe he has also heard about my break up with Rana. I am sure he will never ask me the reason for my sadness, but it will still uplift my spirit. I don't know what went wrong between me and Rana. But I was definitely not comfortable with the boundaries he had set for me. I have always wanted to be free and independent. I tried to save our relationship but it had become toxic. I had to unfortunately quit it before it got worse. I don't want to live in another person's shadow. I want to create my own identity. I want to smile and explore the world. Maybe it is Aarush's influence? He has immensely influenced my life. May this friendship live long! Friendship is always his first choice. At least after months of talking with him, I can draw this conclusion about him. But I haven't been able to make him open up about his life. Questions such as why he was crying that day when we first had our one-to-one conversation still remained largely unanswered.

AARUSH

It was not one of those weekend parties. It was Shivratri. Rishi and Avi had been eagerly waiting for that day. They were ready to unveil their favorite, personal intoxicants. We planned to have lunch by the river Brahmaputra. While we were getting ready in the morning, a message came from the girls' hostel that they wanted to accompany us.

We booked two tempos and set off for the day.

"Aarush, don't forget to collect the bottles from the Rangoli wine shop. We won't be able to carry the bottles on my bike", Avi shouted when we were about to start. I nodded at him.

It was a great day. Everyone had enjoyed to the fullest. "What does this stuff taste like?", Tia asked me.

I smiled at her question. "I don't know. Do you want to try it?"

"Perhaps not", Tia replied. "But I wonder why people are crazy about these things?"

I poured two pegs in a glass and offered it to Tia, "Have it".

"Do you drink?", Tia asked me. She was confused about whether to take the glass or not.

"No, I don't. But you asked me something. To tell you about the taste, I will have to taste it first", I said.

She took the glass reluctantly. She was reacting like someone had given her a glass of rat poison.

"It's coke idiot. Drink it", I assured her. We had a scrumptious lunch later.

In the evening, I could sense some changes in Tia's expression. She was laughing a lot. Though she looked cute, her behaviour seemed a bit strange once we were back in the University campus. I saw her walking towards me wearing an idiotic smile, almost like she was in some kind of trance.

"Hey, are you ok?", Rishi asked Tia.

"Yes, I am alright. Coffee please", she said and took her seat.

"What did you have?", I asked her. I was sure that she had taken something.

"Oh, you don't know? Today is Shivratri", she said and took out some laddoos from her pocket and offered them to us.

"Take this laddoo, nothing will happen. I took some. See I am normal", she continued.

Rishi and I exchanged looks. We figured out what we should do. As Tia continued with her extempore speech, we took her to her hostel. We called Riya, her roommate, to take her safely to her room.

AARUSH

"Hey, happy birthday!", I wished Tia only after the first class was over.

"Thanks, you stupid boy. You are the last one to wish me in the whole class", Tia replied.

I knew it was her birthday. I am very good with remembering special days. I could have wished her at midnight. Even Rishi had wished her at night. I had never wished any girl at night. So, some part of me compelled me to refrain from wishing Tia at night. Soon the second class started. It was economics and every word coming from across the desk sounded like a lullaby. I saw Tia fiddling with her phone. I snatched her phone but had to return it after she gave me a stern look.

After the class, I teased her, "Stop using your mobile in the class."

"Shut up", she said and she left the classroom.

"Hey, what about the treat", I shouted. I was sure Tia heard my words, but she didn't react. I was a bit confused, but I didn't take offence. It was her birthday and she had the right to do what she wanted. Perhaps she needed some time for herself. I stopped thinking about the incident. Anyway, we were scheduled to meet at the cafeteria in the evening for presenting her the customary birthday cake.

Evenings were the best time on the campus. We just loved to hang around in the evening. On the birthday of any one of us, it was like a festival. The amount of chaos we created just amazed the students of the other departments. It seemed like the other animals made room for the lions to have fun.

Rishi and I brought the cake. Everybody was waiting for us. "Hey, are we late?", Rishi asked.

"Nope, dude", It was Avi tuning his guitar.

"The birthday girl is missing", said one of the girls from behind. We did not wait for Tia to begin the fun. Avi started singing his melodies. Rishi started dancing with Riya with that flow. Everyone got busy, and I was standing by the cake, the custodian of the most valuable item of the evening. A few of our friends already started calling her as it was getting late and it was quite difficult to resist the precious cake. Finally, Tia came. She was accompanied by a boy. I heard someone say he was Rana, Tia's boyfriend. Yes, both looked cool. Tia looked stunning in a white salwar suit. Although the visibility was low, I noticed that Tia's smile was missing. Maybe Rana didn't gift what she had demanded. I finally suppressed the pangs of curiosity arising in my brain with this reasoning.

There was music, cake and chicken. We had great fun. And finally, we got ready for the customary walk. The long walks around the campus, those were the precious moments of University life and each one of us enjoyed these moments to the fullest. Those walks included a multitude of things including many arguments, many grudges, misunderstandings, but most importantly bouts of silly laughter and growing bonds of friendship. I came close to Tia and said: “Hey, he is quite handsome.”

She didn’t reply. I was really confused. I wanted to ask her if I had done anything wrong, but again some part of me stopped me from doing so.

I texted her, “Sorry if I have done something wrong or if I have asked something that I shouldn’t have” and headed towards my room.

TIA

I didn't know what was going on in my life. We meet many people in our life. Some of them manage to make a huge impact on us. I recently met one such personality. I thought he might have the answers I was searching for.

I asked, "Why can't we sometimes accept the situations we face?"

"Why should we not accept!", he replied. He continued, "It is a fact that at times we face certain situations and we are not always in a position to control the factors leading to those situations. You can try your best to make things favourable for you. That is in your hand. But the situation may or may not be in your favour. You can do nothing about that, except wait for answers. Whether to wait or not is again your choice as the circumstances might change in the meantime. When we make our choices or try to achieve something, we should be prepared for both the results. And we should accept it gracefully, whether it is in our favour or not".

"But, how can we let go of something special without putting up a fight for it?"

"Who said we shouldn't try? Just don't force things. When we feel some people are special, we love them and we don't want to part with them. But we should also respect their decisions because we love them, even if those decisions are not in our favour.

Nothing is black and white. Grey areas always exist. It is better not to be there for long".

"I agree with your answers but things are not always easy. It's not easy to overcome the grey area between hope and expectations. Forgiving is an easy thing to do, but forgetting things is not always easy. I am ready to accept the present situation gracefully, without any expectation, but I can't stop hoping that things would change in the future. I am trying to forget things and make peace with my reality at present. I know that I have been successful to some extent in my attempts to forget the past, but I don't know whether I am doing the right thing. This process requires me to be submissive and to bury my hopes and expectations. I feel lost. I don't want to challenge the beliefs that I have nurtured for years".

Suddenly, the door opened and he disappeared. I didn't know what that was. How could Aarush be present in my room? I pinched my arm to check if I was dreaming. "Yes, I am real," I said to myself. I felt I needed to talk to someone. The burden of the events happening in my life was crushing me. I picked up my phone and typed "Hey Aarush! Can we meet?" I didn't know what I was for Aarush. Was I a good friend, a classmate, or just an acquaintance? I was confused, but I wanted to be with someone other than myself. I didn't know what he would think. I stopped thinking and pressed the send button.

AARUSH

"Hey, where are you going?", Rishi shouted when I decided to end our Fifa game abruptly. "Sorry, dude! Play in managers' mode for some time. I am just coming", I replied. Rishi hates it when someone leaves a game in Fifa midway. He murmured something to himself as I left. I felt Tia needed me more than Fifa did. I walked out of my room, crossed the long balcony and finally took the route towards the community hall where Tia had summoned me. Though I was a bit nervous and confused, I still felt I should go. I am a strong follower of my heart. Though my mind thought of various reasons for this meeting, I wanted to go to her without any preconceived notions.

When I reached the hall, she was already there. Her Hercules cycle was parked in the basketball court and she was sitting on the platform connected to the stairs. "Come, have a seat", Tia said. I sat near her, on the step below the one she occupied.

We sat there for some time in total silence. It felt like some wizard had transformed us into statues. I was not looking at her eyes, but I could sense that she was disturbed. "So, are you waiting for an auspicious moment to start?", I asked.

She still remained silent. Finally, she said in a very low tone, "I don't know what I should say or why I should say anything."

"It's okay Tia. If you are not comfortable talking about what is bothering you, then take your time. I can wait", I said to her.

"I am not okay Aarush. I just wanted to talk to someone who won't judge me", she said. Tia continued, "I don't know whether what I did is right or wrong, good or bad. I just did it and I don't know what I should feel".

"Hey, there is nothing right or wrong. You need not worry as I won't judge you. You can dump all your emotional baggage on me", I said to her, to reassure her. I didn't know why Tia chose me to tell her story to. But I was amazed by her ability to speak her heart out.

"I was in college when we met for the first time. We were never such close friends but he used to like me. He had proposed to me many times. I didn't know if I loved him or I was just responding to his inclination towards me, but I agreed. It was going all right. He was a confident, good-looking boy and we thought we had a future together. However, gradually, I felt that I was losing the real me. Knowingly or unknowingly, he had set some boundaries for me. At first, I enjoyed them as a part of his love or part of his care. But, as the days passed, it became suffocating. Maybe he was expecting another version of 'me,' not the girl that I really am. The distance between us kept on increasing. Even though we have not split officially, but by now both of us know that it's over.

He still wants me to give our relationship a chance and I thought I was ready for it. But, today he scolded me for clicking photos with you guys. Rana will never change. I don't know Aarush. It's not working", Tia stopped with a long sigh, ending her confession with that long breath.

Her words amplified the intensity of the silence. Both of us remained silent for some time. I was stunned by her words. They rendered me completely speechless and I was at a loss for words.

"So, how do you feel now?", I asked. I didn't know what else to say.

"What do you mean? What am I supposed to feel? I am tense", she said.

Tia was looking cute though she was tense. I could see the stress on her face. She was scratching her scalp. I didn't know what exactly she was feeling, but she was in pain. I wanted to help her. I wanted to console her.

"It's ok, Tia. Nobody's life is perfect and don't think you have done anything wrong. Such problems happen when any relationship is burdened with expectations", I said.

"What do you mean?", Tia asked.

"Nothing, I will explain some other day. Till then keep smiling. You do look better", I said.

"Is it so easy?", Tia questioned.

"Yes! You just bend your lips upward, close your eyes slightly and there you have a smile", I told her, friend to friend. She smiled at my words. I punched her arm, "C'mon, it's your birthday and only two hours are left. Do you want to end your 30th birthday in tears? "

"Shut up! It's my 22ndbirthday", Tia finally smiled. Maybe she didn't smile from the core of her heart, but she smiled.

"And I am sorry for my behaviour on Shivratri. I know I acted like a fool", Tia said.

I smiled at her and said "Yes it was funny, but it's ok. You made many people smile on that day".

"Shut up, I don't know why I strolled out of the hostel that day", she said.

"But I know. You came to give us laddoos", I teased her.

TIA'S DIARY

Sometimes I envy Aarush. I wonder how he manages to maintain his ever-present smile and make people around him happy. He is a real charmer. I don't know whether I did the right thing by telling him my story. But I was quite relieved after speaking to him. Sometimes, it becomes necessary to share ones' disturbing thoughts with others. I too want to smile. I want to get rid of my tears. And I could think of only one person: Aarush. I know he will never judge people. Maybe I have found a friend for life. His presence makes me feel relaxed. He is like the sunshine. There may be clouds that hide the sunshine but beyond it, it's always there. A happy soul. But what did he hint at that night? Maybe he also has something to share and he has not found the right person. I need to know his story. I need to know things like why he was crying when we had met the other day. I wonder if there is any story beyond his smiling face. But, he can always smile. "Keep smiling! It is the best medicine", he had told me once. I still remember. And now, I mostly wear a fake smile. I long for that "best medicine". The smile that was genuine and went beyond the lips. Somewhere straight to my heart.. I wish I could go back to a time when I could effortlessly smile. I have stored every beautiful moment of my life that is close to my heart. I would like to believe that every person close to my heart will always remember me. I make an effort towards this end. I know that it should be an effortless process. Sometimes, I think I should have been more practical. I should have let myself move on. But from where to where? My world is not about forgetting people. I believe in preserving the beautiful things that life has gifted me. Otherwise, there will be nothing left. I have lost so much while trying to hold on to everything. Now I am scared to create any new memory. I fear the moment may turn into a horror story in no time. I tried, but I failed many times and I feel sorry for myself, for not being able to keep myself happy.

AARUSH

The clock was yet to strike six in the morning when I started my morning walk. Tia's story was still in my mind. Perhaps, she came one step closer to my heart. She was a person I would be happy to treasure my whole life. But she didn't deserve the tears. She was a dreamer yet she was grounded; a believer yet practical; complicated yet simple. I had also seen her fragile side that night. I wanted to give her a hug, like my mom used to give me. It always works. At least I liked to believe that it did. I wanted to see her happy.

"Hey, wait for me", a voice called out to me from the distance. I stopped on hearing the voice coming from a distance. It was Tia.

"Hi, what are you doing? By the way, good morning!", I greeted her. Her smile was still missing. It was the first time I observed her from such close quarters,. The mole on the right side of her nose, her tiny black eyes. It seemed she was still in a lot of pain.

"Good morning! Can I walk with you?", Tia asked. We started walking together. The campus was always beautiful and after the rain last night, it had come alive.

"You walk every morning?", Tia asked.

"Yes! I love mornings and evenings and I don't want to miss them. Initially, I used to jog to my football practice. But now I just walk. Why should we waste our time thinking about whether to do something or not, especially when we like to do that particular thing?", I said. Tia only replied "hmm..." in response, to my words. Her mind was still preoccupied. But I didn't ask anything. It's not healthy to talk about the negative things in life.

"So, what about you?", I asked.

"Mornings bring freshness. The sun never complains or refuses to rise in the morning. It is always so punctual. I want to love and live these moments", Tia said.

I smiled at her words and asked, "Why are you impressed at someone's punctuality?", Tia was confused with my question. Maybe she never reflected on what she was saying. She just went with the flow.

"Don't think so much Tia. Life is easy if you think it's easy. Just live in the moment. You are still 25. You have so many things to do", I said.

"Shut up! I said I am 22", she smiled meekly.

"Yes! Good try", I thought.

"So, we are good friends now?", she asked. I was a little surprised by the sudden change of topic. I tried to figure out where she was heading. I nodded with a smile though.

"I want to know your story", she said.

I laughed and said, "I am an open book".

"No, Aarush. I want to know why you were crying when we had met that day. I know you have something to tell and I am here to listen to you", she said. I was confused. I know I was dealing with disturbing thoughts and sometimes wanted to talk to someone more than anything else. But, how could she have found out? I wondered, "Am I so vulnerable?" I was not used to sharing my stories. I liked to keep them to myself. Nobody completely understands someone else's story until he or she has been through the same situation. But I felt inclined to share my story with Tia.

AARUSH: The Night

I got the call before nine in the evening. After a busy and joyful day, it was time for the finance assignments. With music competitions going on in full swing at the community hall, we were just trying to wrap up the assignments as quickly as humanly possible. These early hours in the evening are my personal favourite. Slightly distracted, "Okay", I responded to my father's call in the midst of loud, musically tuned noise. Still, I could make out that he was asking me to visit home once. He was speaking in his usual voice but I was just perplexed at his proposal. In my last six or seven years, away from home, he has never requested me to come home. My mother always hung up the phone after enquiring when I would next come home. I rushed to my room, as a deep void began engulfing my mind. In spite of being disoriented, I rightly guessed that the call had something to do with my mom. I wondered if I had been summoned home because of her upcoming health check-up in Delhi. I decided to travel in the morning. Thanks to my hostel mates who insisted that I go right away, I reconsidered my decision. I was just confused and could not think straight. Rishi and Avi arranged for Riyan's car to drop me somewhere near the highway. I did not have any idea of what was going on around me. I reached the bus stop in the town around 11 at night, accompanied by Rishi, Avi and Riyan. Everything seemed weird. My call to the Dean and the decision of travelling at night and then, taking help from Riyan. Finally, around 11:20 p.m., a bus appeared and I managed to get a seat in the driver's cabin. I was used to travelling at night and so it was not a big deal. But the call from Rishi, when I was almost halfway, put me in a very awkward situation. They were going to drop me. I felt pretty bad that I couldn't convince them otherwise. I went with the flow and they drove me to my brother's place. It was 3 a.m. when we entered my brother's house. I just had nothing to say except thanking them for the help. My mind was loaded with many questions. I didn't know what to surmise from the sense of urgency. Finally, I accepted the situation at hand and settled in my brother's bed. I was completely unaware of what was going to happen. Reaching my brother's place at odd hours was not new to me. His usual expressionless face allowed me to ignore him and helped me to take a short nap.

I was woken up before 3:30 a.m. My brother insisted on catching the morning ferry that carries newspapers to my hometown in the early morning. His friend took us to Nimati ghat. My home is in Majuli, surrounded by the mighty Brahmaputra River. Nimati ghat, a dock, was the only gateway to my homeland. With a sweater adorning my body and a muffler around the neck, I was shielded well against the cold. I fell back on my seat and closed my eyes. The view outside was still unclear due to the darkness and the fog. After several minutes of darkness, a ray of reddish light appeared in the east, piercing the darkness. We soon reached the dock and I stepped out of the car. The cold outside was quite unwelcoming.

The ferry kept us waiting for over an hour. A very restless hour. Finally, around 6 a.m., we boarded the ferry and bade farewell to my brother's friend. The small ferry was fast enough to cross the Brahmaputra river within 30 minutes. In the meantime, my brother made a few calls. I didn't find any reason to inquire about the calls. He was perhaps arranging for bikes to go home. I wanted to believe that things were fine, although everything about this time felt very strange. As we reached the dock, I saw two bikes awaiting us. I didn't question anybody. Everything was happening so dramatically that I could hardly talk.

Finally, we rode through the lane leading to our house. I could sense that things were weird. Everyone passing by looked at us with sympathetic eyes. Now, I was at home. Everyone was crying. I discovered the truth that I was trying to avoid. My dearest friend, the only lady in my life, my mother was no more. She couldn't even say her final goodbye to me.

TIA

I staggered on hearing Aarush's story. I knew he had lost his mother. I felt guilty. Maybe I should not have asked, I felt like I had renewed his pain. What a fool I was! He was still by my side, walking slowly. I wanted to console him. We both kept walking silently. I was lost in my thoughts. His pain was much deeper than mine. Still, he kept his smile alive and continued spreading happiness among his friends.

"Tea or coffee?", a voice called out to me. I came back to reality with Aarush's question and never noticed we reached the main gate of the University.

"Aarush, thank you!", I said.

"But I haven't paid yet", he smiled at me. His eyes were saying a lot.

"You know what I mean. Anyways, let us have the cup of that tea that you love", I said and took our seat by the tea stall. His smile was still there. I could never imagine Aarush without a smiling face.

"Aarush, I am sorry for your loss", I said. He was still smiling.

"You don't need to be sorry", he replied. His nature always surprises me. His ability to deal with situations. His control over his temper sometimes makes me jealous. I can't imagine a day without my mom and he is sitting by my side so calm, so composed.

"You loved your mom right?", I asked.

"No, I still love her. Her presence or absence doesn't affect my love for her", he responded without hesitation.

"But why were you crying?", I again raised the question. The question I had always been curious about.

"Is crying a crime?", he counter questioned. I had no answer. I felt crying is a punishment.

"It's ok. If you feel like crying, cry. That means, your tears are loyal to you. You can't fake a tear. It always carries emotions. So it's more real than a smile. Sometimes it's essential to express your emotions. People you love may not always be with you. That doesn't mean they do not love you", he said.

"How can you always wear your smile?", I asked.

"Why should I cry? What complaints should I raise! Life has given me many reasons to be happy", he was still replying with the same intensity.

"Did you cry for your mom?", I blurted out. I didn't understand why I asked that stupid question. I immediately tried to rectify my mistake, "Sorry! It's a bad question".

"No, it's ok. I can understand why you are asking. Actually, I cried initially, and then...", he paused, rather unnaturally. The curious side of me was eagerly waiting for his next words. I could not resist myself, "Then what?"

"Hey, you are always in a hurry. Then what... maybe my tears ran out of stock", he smiled. It was not so funny, but I too joined him. I could sense he was avoiding some part of the story.

"And why are you always behind my smile or tear? There are lots of things you can enjoy in this beautiful world. Every day God will give you reasons to smile, to create moments that you will be happy to keep safely in your heart", he told me. Yes, he was right. I was lost somewhere in the past. I had stopped chasing my dreams. I had stopped being me and I had lost my smile. I desperately wanted it back.

"Can I smile too?", I whispered but he heard it clearly. He smiled at my question.

"Yes, obviously! Everyone should smile", he said.

"But, I am unable to get rid of my past. It is still haunting me", I said without considering what he would think. After a long silence, I said, "Sorry! It's my problem, forget it".

Then, he spoke, "See Tia, I don't know what happened between you and Rana. I give due respect to the privacy that my friends deserve. So you can speak out your mind. And I have never been in love so I can't feel your pain, but I can feel the pain of losing the people close to your heart. Being in the shadow of sadness is not an option. And don't expect me to speak anything about your relationship because I am not competent enough to talk about that. But I assure you, being a friend, you will always find me standing with you."

The conversation was turning a bit serious. I felt he wanted to say something more. But I said, "Should I regret the choice I made?!" I ended it with a short pause.

"Let me tell you something. The day before my mom's demise, she had called me twice, but I didn't answer the calls, intentionally. The first call came when I was busy with finance assignments and the second call came when I was watching the music competition and nothing was audible in the community hall. I was supposed to call her back. But I never did. I cried many times for not responding to her phone call. I was too busy to attend the last phone call", he confessed and he sighed after saying those words. I could feel his pain. I wanted to give him a hug to console him. For a while, I forgot all my pain. I wanted to cry for him. Sometimes, small things impact our lives so deeply that it takes years to overcome the loss.

"I am sorry about that", I said.

"No, you do not need to be sorry. Now I don't cry, but every day I live with her love. I can't talk to her now, but her voice is still alive in my mind. Her love did not end with her departure", Aarush said with a smile but I could sense it was ingrained with deep, underlying emotions. I could understand his love for his mother, and what he lost was not even comparable to my situation.

"In your case, I can only say one thing: expectations ruin relations. Everyone is beautiful in their own way and nobody is perfect. Sometimes, we need to do little adjustments to create happy moments for us and that's ok", he continued. "See Tia, in life we always make choices. Life is full of possibilities and brimming with options. We can't choose everything. So, the risk of missing out on one possible option is always there. Just follow your heart. The brain may give you the logical decision, but the heart always gives you the right decision. And at the end of the day, it's your heart that suffers not the brain", he laughed while giving that answer.

I went into deep thought with his words. He had also faced something similar to what I was facing. But he was so composed, so clear about his thoughts. On the other hand, I felt so fragile. I came back to my senses with his punch on my right arm.

"Hey, let's go. Its late", he said. I did not object. We went through the main gate and parted on our way to our respective hostels.

AARUSH'S DIARY

I hate it when someone looks at me with sympathy. Maybe that's why I don't like sharing my personal life with others. I like to be loved and I have always done everything in my capacity to earn the love of the people around me. My best buddies, and my family. I don't know why I went on speaking about my life with this girl. But truly, she is a girl with determination. She can put an end to her relationship with a special person if the relationship is causing any problem in her life. A brave decision. Maybe I would have never done that. But she needs to get her smile back. I want to help her. Yes, she is one of my best buddies. I feel like it is my duty to make her happy. My feelings for her are platonic. She is just a very good friend.

TIA

It was a lazy morning and I was still in my bed. I checked my email as always and noticed a new message from Aarush. It contained one attachment.

Love is all around you

Your dream is your hope

Take what you need dear

Take what you need

Don't rush for the peace

Don't come to a cease

Keep faith in God

And patience in you

Take what's best for you dear

Take what you need

Don't be scared

Be brave and move on

Appreciate the life

It's not what you see

Come to the light

Take what you need

World is filled with beauty

Take time to glance around

Come out of your own shadow

Everything that you need is free.

A smile flashed across my face. What a beautifully written poem! Aarush was really cool. I felt lucky to have a friend like him. It seemed like it was meant for me. Every word represented my situation so accurately. I took my cell phone and unlocked my screen. One unread message from Aarush; "Rise and shine. Good morning". I was impressed by the care he shows to his friends, not only to me. I have seen the way he treats Rishi and Avi. He never thinks twice before helping them.

AARUSH

"What's up, friend?", I asked Tia on our way to the department. She smiled back at me. She looked awesome in her blue saree. Tia was walking to the department. So I got down from the cycle and joined her. It was the first day of our campus interview. Yes Bank was conducting the interview for the post of assistant manager.

"You are looking beautiful", I admired her.

"Oh, thanks! It's my mom's saree. You know, interview special saree", she said.

"Ok, well prepared?", I asked.

"Yes, I would like to believe so. Anyway, I won't regret if they don't select me", I was a bit confused by her answer.

"Wait, what are you saying? You are a finance student", I tried to find out something more.

"Actually, I want to go explore, become a traveler, I don't want to be in a bank, counting others' money", she said. I found her words fascinating. But before an interview, what was she doing? "Oh ho! I appreciate your thoughts. But still, good luck for the interview. We can discuss this in the evening", I said. By the time we reached our department, everything was set for the interview. All finance students stayed back and I went to the class.

We were scheduled to meet in the evening. I already got the news. She was not selected. She was there before time, sitting alone in the shopping complex. I reached there before my usual schedule because she wanted to meet early.

"So the gypsy rejected the bank job", I said. She was a bit disappointed, I noticed. It was clearly visible in her eyes.

"Shut up! They rejected me. I don't know what will happen to me", she said.

"Oh sorry about that. But life always gives us another chance. And moreover, it was our first campus interview", I tried to console her.

"By the way, your parents are scheduled to come here today, right?", I asked

"Yes, but they have cancelled their visit. Papa got stuck in the office, and...", she stopped after 'and'. I waited for a while, but nothing came out of her mouth.

"And?", I enquired.

"Forget it. It is not relevant now. I wanted a bank challan for filling up my NET form. It's with him and he couldn't make it", she said.

I didn't ask anything else about her challan and focused on being familiar. "It's ok, tea or coffee?"

"I just had a cup of tea", she said. I asked her, "Why are you so afraid of the future?"

Tia seemed confused. She seemed completely unprepared for that kind of question, perhaps she was unaware of the fact that she was afraid of the future.

"Because the future is uncertain", she murmured meekly.

"I am not afraid of the future. I just want to see my parents happy. What will people say if I sit jobless after my MBA?", I laughed at her answer.

"Stop laughing! I will kill you", she slapped me teasingly.

"What do you dream of doing in your future? Apart from driving in your friend's Ferrari to the dhaba?", she smiled.

"Who thinks so much about the future? Live the moment, Tia. You just missed the taste of the cup of tea for this euphoria called future", I smiled at her to remind her of her own intentions with life.

"I wish I could be like you", she said.

"You can be better than me. You are far more determined and focused than me and you will definitely fly high", I assured her.

"Aren't you scared of the future?", Tia asked. I wanted to say how much I was scared of the future, of losing people. But before I could reply other members of our class joined us for evening tea and put an end to the conversation.

AARUSH

It was drizzling outside. I went out of my room and knocked on Avi's door. "Hey Avi, It's me, Aarush". I could sense that Avi was not very pleased with being woken up so early. But I knew Avi, an enthusiast biker, was the right guy for this job.

"Let's go for a bike ride", I suggested.

"Are you mad? It's not even six in the morning", he groaned. I felt the urgency of that ride. I had to convince him. So I asked him, "Ok then, and give me your bike. I will go alone".

"Ok, give me 10 minutes. I am coming. You go and prepare the bike", he replied. I knew he would never give me the keys of his new Royal Enfield.

When we left the campus, it was still drizzling and we hit the road pretty soon. After riding for 15 minutes, I asked him to take a right turn. He became curious and asked, "Where are we heading?"

"Tia's home!", I said loudly. He stopped the bike on hearing those words.

"Are you crazy? It's too early to visit someone and look at my clothes. And on top of that, it's a girl's home", Avi reacted furiously.

"It's ok, but this is important. Please!", J said. He agreed on the term that I would buy him 500 bucks worth of petrol. Finally, we did it.

AARUSH'S DIARY

It was insane. I have never done something like this in my life. That too, for a girl! Is this only because I want to see her happy? Yes, I want to convince myself that we are only friends, nothing more than that. Her friendship has been a precious addition to my life. The void my mom had left in my heart seemed to heal after her arrival. And I don't want to ruin our relationship by burdening it with expectations;. I can't love her. Expectations always kill relationships. I recently lost someone dear to me and I can't afford to go through it once more. She is a girl with wings and I enjoy being on the ground. Friendship is the only possibility between us. I just want to be friends; a friend forever without expectations.

TIA'S DIARY

I was surprised when Aarush gave me the challan after the first class. But, how did he bring it? When did he bring it? I had told him about it only 13 hours earlier. This boy is crazy. But, most importantly, why did he do it? For a friend or for someone else? I was scared by the second option. I won't be able to say no if someday, he proposes to me. But I don't want to bind him with my choices, my dreams. He is a happy soul. He deserves someone better;. someone who could love him without any fear.

From my most recent relationship, I have learnt that talking to your close ones is important. You need to communicate what you feel, whatever you are planning or envisioning with him or her.

I learnt that when someone close to your heart has some problem, you should meet the person. Physical presence matters a lot.

I learnt that nothing is permanent. So you should take very good care of the things you love. Not everyone is lucky to get a second chance.

I learnt that you should not be overconfident. It really kills a relationship.

I learnt that sometimes you just can't forget some memories because those memories are so close to your heart that if you try to scratch them out, it bleeds.

Waiting is a mixture of smiles and tears. You smile when you think something good can happen, and when you realize the amount of time that goes by as you wait for it to happen, sadness persists. There is another word associated with it and that is hope. Hope for something good, for happiness, for a better tomorrow. But for now, I don't want Aarush to get hurt because of me. I can't afford to lose our precious friendship. We will soon leave this place after the completion of the course. I have to hold on to it till then. Remember, just friends.

AARUSH

Finally, the day that I wished would never come was at here. It was time to bid farewell. By that time, we all were emotional. It was an informal session. We all gathered on the rooftop of our department to share our thoughts. Everyone spoke a few lines. It was our last week at this University. After that, nobody knew where he or she would land up. "Aarush, say something", said someone from behind, reminding me that now it was my turn. I collected my thoughts.

"I have many thoughts but because of my poor writing and speaking skills , I often feel handicapped. During my school days, I used to be a silent boy and never a salient part of my so-called friends circle. When I went for my senior secondary classes, I felt lost. No doubt, I had or rather have very good friends from senior secondary, but I realized that I have missed out on many things. I tried to look back at my school days and by God's grace, there was still room for me to enter those memories. Now I am no more a silent boy.At least, I think I am better than before. And I think I am already in the circle. The circle formed of the closest of friends'. With time some points in the circumference may vanish but I hope that time never comes. These two years brought about many changes in me. Obviously, some are visible and some are not so visible. While in university, I have learned many things, and many a time I could smile only because of you people. Sometimes, the Almighty takes away our loved ones much sooner than we ever thought. And there are

some moments, when you miss someone so much that you wish you could take them out of your imagination and see them for real. Keeping aside the dreams, we manage to hope, we aspire, and we smile together. I tried to go with the flow of life to match with the changing circumstances. 2011 brought the beginning. 2013 brings the end and somewhere in the middle, we became friends. Thanks for being with me, for making me a better person. You all will be safely stored in my heart. This is probably going to be the last weekend at this university. Unlike any other Friday, it doesn't come with assignments. So, theoretically, I should be happy and relaxed. But that is not how I feel and so I want to pause time. I try to stay awake so as to not waste these precious moments. During the early days of my student life, I had a secret desire. I wanted to get rid of studies as soon as possible. Now when my formal education wants to bid me farewell, I just don't want to accept it. This surely is going to be the first occasion when the end of an examination is going to make me sad. It seems like this examination has summoned us just to give us another reason to hate it. Still, I would be happy to appear in hundreds of exams if time promises that it will slow down. We cheated. We lied. We fought over stupid things. We stayed up late at night to have deep conversations. We hated some for no reason and sometimes we ended up getting hurt. Maybe one day, these memories will make me cry. Crying does not mean a person is weak. Sometimes it means that the person has a heart. I am thankful to God for giving me all these precious moments because of which I am finding it very hard to say good bye"

We were all very emotional that day. I had landed a job with a logistics company; so I would soon shift to Ahmadabad. Rishi had been selected for a bank in Kolkata. Avi would be working for an FMCG company at Guwahati. And Tia, she was yet to be selected. I really wanted her to get a job, a really good job. I wanted to speak to her, wanted to say that this is the moment I always feared. I wanted to go back in time, when our classes had just started. I wanted to relive the moments once more. Some of the best days of our lives were coming to an end. Everyone seemed filled to the brim with memories that they had sealed within themselves for eternity. Everyone seemed ready to move forward in search of a bright career. Still, I don't want to move on. The overpriced food items of the shopping complex, bunking classes, late submission of assignments and that necessary Monday formalwear. Every little thing seemed so important for me today. Some of the facilities will continue to be here but this group of students, sitting at the complex, waiting for the VC to go. Yes, the group was about to be scattered. I wish that everything worked like machines. At least they would have come with a pause button. I wanted to hold on to these days at University so tight that it hurts real bad. Now, it's almost the end of our journey and we can afford to have selfish thoughts. I just wasn't ready to say good bye.

"Hey, are you going to tell your real feelings to Tia today? Look, she is coming", said Avi. Since I took him to Tia's home that morning, he has been after me. I saw her. I have never seen such a beautiful girl. A smile flashed across my face on seeing Tia.

"Shut up. We are friends", I replied. But I was unsure if my feelings for Tia were limited to the zone of "just friends". Are we just friends?

"Hey, who told you that you are a bad speaker?", Tia said.

"I don't know. I never spoke in public, so I thought maybe I am not good", I replied. She was still smiling.

"Will you miss me?", she asked. I wanted to shout out to the crowd about my feelings, how badly I was going to miss Tia. But some part of me still restricted me. "Maybe, I will miss everything here and you are not an exception", I said. "Will you miss me when you will be out exploring the world? When you will be at the highest point of the world", I continued.

Tia paused for a while "No, I won't because I doubt I will ever make it to Everest", she smiled. I joined her. "I love you", I said in my mind. But I couldn't muster the courage to say it loud. "What did you say?", Tia asked. I was sweating. Did she hear what I said? But I never said it aloud. I stammered. "Nothing, maybe I just said that I love tea. Can we have one in the evening?"

She laughed at my reactions. "Yup, sure", she replied.

TIA'S DIARY

Though I wanted to hear those words from him, still I was scared. I heard him saying those words. Maybe my inner desires tricked me into hearing those words. I don't know what is happening. Maybe I will regret my choice, but I will have to stick to my decision. I don't want to make Aarush's life miserable. I owe him my smile when I could not find anyone by my side, he was there, both physically and mentally. Since I discovered him as a friend, I have never felt alone in this crowded University. I know he has started liking me, but I don't want him to love me. I won't be able to bear the weight of his love. And I don't want to burden him with my past. I can't be so selfish and hurt this guy. I still have to write this diary. The diary I am planning to gift him as a parting gift. I will pen down some of my innermost feelings in that diary and gift him. The diary would be my farewell gift to my best friend, just my best friend. We are nothing more than that. Let's see how much I can write.

TIA

"Hey, wake up", someone said on the other side of the phone. It took me a minute to recognize that it was Aarush. It was cold. Maybe it was raining outside. This guy is crazy. Who calls so early in the morning?

"What?", I replied reluctantly.

"Come out. I will take you to Everest", he said.

What rubbish was he saying? I was annoyed as he was disturbing my sleep.

"Come. I am waiting at your hostel gate", he said. "What? Are you mad? Ok wait, I am coming", I almost shouted at him. I took my umbrella and rushed to the gate. He was there waiting with his bicycle.

"Hey, good morning", he wished me as soon as I reached the gate.

"What's good about this morning, and what are you doing in this rain?", I said.

"Shut up and sit". He threw away my umbrella and ordered me to take the back seat of his cycle. I did not rationalize what I was doing. I just followed what he was saying.

"So, we are going to Mount Everest on your cycle", I mocked him.

"Please keep quiet for the next 10 minutes", he said. I did so. My heart started beating fast. But I didn't say anything. I left everything up to destiny. We crossed the VC's bungalow, our department and then finally he stopped his cycle.

"I hope you are not afraid of heights", he said and then continued cycling. I was confused.

Then we stopped by the water tank. We started climbing. I asked, "What if we are seen by some professor or guard?", I asked, worried. "Shut up! Who cares? Today we will leave this place forever, so just do it", he commanded.

Finally, we reached the top. Lush green fields, newly constructed buildings, everything was distinct. The rain just added to the beauty. "It's beautiful", I said.

"Yes, I know, sometimes we overlook the beauty surrounding us," he said.

"I never thought our campus could have such a view", I said

"Tia, every moment of life, every place can be made beautiful, we just need beautiful eyes to look at it and the right company by our side. We can't have everything at the same time. We can't be everywhere, so it's better we try to enjoy the things we have", he said in his usual thoughtful way. After enjoying the moment for some time, we decide to get down. Aarush just added one more memorable moment to my life. I might one day reach great heights, but I doubt I would be able to enjoy as much as I did with him. That was not less than Everest. On the way back, I gave him the diary I had written for him. "Around 2 p.m., my parents will come and I will leave with them", I said. I asked if he would come to see me.

He paused and said, "I can't say. I have plans to go to town by the 2:30 bus". He left the place abruptly. I could feel he was holding back his tears. His tears were too loyal to him.

TIA'S DIARY

Aarush, my friend,

You are such a sweetheart. I guess nobody will dare to deny that statement.

I think everyone has already used all the adjectives in the world to describe you. So, there is nothing much left for me to add. I need to invent some new ones. This University has given me many memories, bitter as well as sweet and you know everything. But the sweetest gift of all that this University has given me is you. You are very special to me. I never thought that I would find such a good friend in you. Your friendship is precious enough to treasure for life. I don't know how it all started. Perhaps, I always knew that behind that veil of indifference, there is a sweet little boy, craving for love. Friendship is all he wants. He can do anything for his friends and can never hurt anyone. And I hope by now, I am also among your friends. I have witnessed your transformation from being "not noticed" to being "hard not to notice". Your absence is felt whenever you are not there. Your smile will forever be intact in my memory. I don't know why I have this faith in you. You know, I sincerely admire you. How can you be so selfless? And believe me you have inspired me to be a good human being. Thank you for everything. Thank you for being there for me every time. For listening to me and thank you for making me smile whenever I felt low and down.

And last but not the least, thanks for being so sweet. You are so sweet that anybody would fall in love with you. Perhaps if I didn't have my past to deal with, I would also have fallen in love with you. Nevertheless, I still love you as my friend. I just pray to God that he blesses you with a wonderful life partner, one who can understand your emotions and help you lead a blissful life. The girl who marries you has to be one of the luckiest girls.

Your friend,

Tia

AARUSH

I read the diary soon after I reached my room. I was not sure when I would be able to see her. The familiar pain of losing someone close to me was clawing at my heart once again. I wanted to cry. I wanted to shout and I wanted to tell her that I loved her. I was lying on my bed like a dead man.

"Aarush, Tia's parents have arrived. Let's go", Rishi and Avi came to take me to the girl's hostel. I dressed up and took my seat on Avi's bullet. We planned to go to town after seeing her off. When we reached, many girls were there too. Some of them were crying. Tia came to us and hugged Avi.

"Hey, stay connected", Avi said.

"Yes, I will", she replied. Then it was Rishi's turn and when she stood in front of me, I offered my hand and shook her hand. She was smiling but she had tears in her eyes. "You love tea, right? Someday I will make you a cup of tea", she said. She nodded and said "Bye."

I didn't wait there. I rushed to the bus stop and waited for the bus. I was overwhelmed with emotions when the bus came. I saw that Tia was sitting next to the window. I couldn't believe myself. We exchanged smiles and I took another seat although the seat next to her was vacant. What a fool I was! I should have understood why she decided to catch the bus instead of going with her parents. I was dying to take the seat by her, but I never did.

Finally, the bus stopped at the highway. She got down there. I followed her, but she disappeared. I wasn't brave enough to call her at that time. I took the next bus to the campus and got lost in the emotions that I was already finding too heavy to carry.

TIA'S NOTEBOOK

I can't do this. I have started having feelings for Aarush. And I know he also feels the same way. Maybe he will never propose to me. It's better for us to take a break. In friendship, one can easily control any damage that occurs because friends always forgive. I am scared to step into his life and complicate it. One day, maybe I won't be able to justify why, but I am unable to do it now. So, goodbye, my dearest sweetheart. And I am sorry, but I can't say goodbye to you. I wish I could explain to him my decision.

AARUSH

Tia left for Delhi seven days after our last meeting. I left for Ahmadabad, three weeks after she left. She never called me. I had her number and I believe she also had mine. But her name never popped up on the screen of my phone. Keep smiling. It is said that smiling is the best medicine. And nowadays that "best medicine" is missing from my life or rather the connection between my heart and the "medicine" is missing. I wish I could go back to a time when I could smile effortlessly. I have religiously stored every beautiful moment close to my heart. I like to believe that every person close to my heart will always remember me. And I make an effort to ensure that they do not forget me. I know it should be an effortless process, but still... And I haven't found any reason to complain till date. When I look back, I wonder if I should have been more practical. If I should have moved on. But from where to where? My world is not about forgetting people. I believe in holding on to the beautiful things that life has gifted me. If I let go of the things from my past which I value, I will be left with nothing. I have lost many things while trying to hold on to everything. Now I am scared of creating new memories. I felt like apologizing to myself for not being able to keep smiling. She was gone. I just wanted to confess how much I loved her. I wanted to say I made a wrong choice. When something is broken, it subsequently loses its beauty. So true, perhaps... Though I promised not to get attached to anything or anyone, it was not an easy task. I had cocooned my heart well so that it stayed safe; so that it didn't come into conflict with my life. We try to protect our heart because we don't want our teardrops to betray us. We like to be in control of our emotions. I too am possessive about my heart and want to protect it from being broken into pieces. My heart has been in my control for years now, but I have lost it. Now it doesn't listen to me. Like a spoilt son of a rich man, it has started doing things which I would have never allowed it to do. Sometimes the price of a thing doesn't matter, but the memories associated with those things do matter a lot. I didn't want to replace my memories of Tia with new memories because the new memories might give me some comfort but it will never be the same. I will not be able to associate the new memories with the past moments that I cherish. Time has taught me that everything in life is not replaceable. We need to safeguard certain things. Some things we need to protect. Sometimes we need to say out loud.

Yes, I love her.

Never felt like this before,

Now I know how it feels

To have a broken heart,

Dreamt of a long journey

Supposed to travel

Now I know how it feels

To travel a journey alone,

Roaming around strange paths
Kept on searching for a familiar face
Now I know how it feels
To rest in an unknown place.
I lost my way dear
Please hold my hands
I am about to fall
Please don't leave me alone
I know you have
Chosen your path
And you will be happy again
Now I know how it feels
Yes it feels like
A nail in the heart
Please listen to the prayers
In my cry
Please hold me firm
Show me the way

AARUSH: THE LAST 3 YEARS

"Tears taught me that she is important,

Sleepless nights taught me that she is my dream,

The pain taught me that I am not complete without her

Then the eyes said please take me to her I just one to see her

The heart shouted don't let her go, I am connected to her…

The brain said you are fool, she is gone…"

A STALKER:

"The idea of "she is gone" was very devastating for me. Every night just before falling into deep slumber, weird thoughts flashed across my mind. And most of the times, it started with 'why?' 'Why it happened?' 'Why I couldn't stop her?' 'Why it happened to me?' etc. That small collection of 'Why's of my personal dossier, sometimes lead to other thoughts and those were from the future. Yes, it's a heart, and I knew it couldn't be forced. And when its going mad, just let it free. Let it go beyond everything. "I hope, one day, it will take rest. I hope one day it will rediscover something where it will stay". And I kept thinking, but the truth was just because you called didn't mean the other one has to answer. And just because you showed up didn't mean that person had to welcome you. You can just wait and wait. Sometimes it can be stressful, sometimes it can be beautiful and sometimes it just a way to pass the time. That's what a wait is. It had been years. I was unable to see my best friend. "

I was relocated to Lucknow from Ahmedabad. Many times, I tried to meet her, but things were not so simple. Try was a very controversial word to be used exactly. My new address gave me luxury to visit Delhi on the weekends. A chaotic city and some unknown corner of that city was the home of my heartbeat. Proximity made me do stupid things. One fine morning, I ended up in front of the huge office. Obviously I was not dressed properly to get a free pass to the campus of the company. I waited the whole day only to see a glance of her in the evening. She, along with her colleagues, took a walk to catch the metro and I was standing a few meters away. I wanted to call her, but I couldn't. At that moment, I was both happy and scared. Happy because I could have a clear view of my love and scared because what she would think if she discovered what I was doing.

CONFUSIONS: LOVE, LIFE AND WAITS...

Everything will get boring one day. Love or friendship or family or may be any other relationship isn't only a feeling, nor a commitment to love every day. 100% physically and emotionally. It's not always about the laughs, the smile or the fun. And it's obvious that people tend to quit when it stops being easy. "The spark is gone". Like a potential good day is just covered by the dark clouds. And people tend not to wait till the sun defeat clouds. Yes! Some people call it being practical. No, I don't think that is how it works. We need someone to never give up on us. And I decided to wait.

Someone might have said, "Follow your heart but take your brain with you". Sounds very rational and logical but sometimes it becomes quite impractical too. Main reason behind the impracticality, because in the normal state, we generally ignore this kind of sentences. What decides our happiness, or state of mind? If it is the brain, then why does the heart feel? The situation sometimes may put you in such a position, neither can your brain can decide the right choice, nor does your heart know what is right. Then we prefer following the timeline. Tiktok. Days and nights. And one fine day, we ask why we are suffering when nothing was in our hand. We all have the time to regret but it's of no use. Already, the situation has done a lot to you. Ironically, our brain understands it but the heart many-a times refused to understand.

It hurts. Yes, when I was asked what you feel about love. These are the two words came out of my mind. Is it useless to get attached to people? It was a serious amusement, I thought. The representation of the oxymoronic moments of my recent past. What is good isn't important any more. What is right doesn't mean anything. It's always a blurred zone of mindset persists. But what's profit? Or better, what's the take away from the situations? Perhaps negative. Perhaps consequences are more unfavorable. But again, the question is "does anyone really care?" Again the same you will find itself in a blank situation. Looking for known names, if they care or not. Expecting someone close to heart to care, to ask you one of the most common questions of conversation "How are you?" When the question comes from that person, I feel like my sadness will be blown away soon.

Love is a difficult game to play. Each possible move represents a different game. Every different decision you take can lead you a completely different world. One common thing is that in each of those possible decisions, there is a hope. Life has nothing to offer if it doesn't have any hope. Even if it seems life is too risky, any move can be bad. But there is virtually infinite number of ways to find a way out. Simply if you make a mistake, there are infinite ways to fix it. So, there is always hope. The grief from the past is real. The moments you want to remember for life are also real. Life is real when there is a hope.

I never wanted to be a stalker or a cheap "*ashiq*" type of boy, but every time I looked at her, her achievements, her life style and my nature, it all reacted in favour of my quietness. I became dumb all those years. I had her number but could never gather the courage to dial the number. I always had her address but never had the courage to write to her. The wait has always been a mixture of smiles and tears. I often cursed myself for the inability to speak my heart out in the first place.

CHASING NOTHING:

Who doesn't like to dream? Or the more appropriate question will be, who doesn't dream? Everyone loves to dream. Some are focused, some are realistic, and some are just carefree regarding those dreams. Everyone has a different attitude. And some are insanely emotional. Nevertheless, it is the dreams that fuel our lives to struggle, to fight and most of the times, just to muster the necessary energy to live another day because of the attachment with those dreams. But the question echoed, "Am I chasing nothing?" Maybe be I am actually chasing nothing. Maybe I am totally unsure about the path leading to my dreams. I remembered instances when I ran against the time to make things happen. I saw moments challenging my happiness. I witnessed smiles fading away… and those were the moments when I regret for not chasing those moments down. Life moves either fast or slow, but it never halts. Maybe life itself is a race where no one gets nothing in the end. But nobody has seen the end yet. It may be painful. It may be shameful. Still, I dream. I want to chase. Maybe I am chasing after nothing. But still, they are my dreams and they help me to smile. They persuade me to live one more day with hope, with a smile.

Six months ago, with the same hope, I went to Airport. Thanks to social media, I could easily find her arrival date from Mumbai. Hopeful, the stalker me couldn't ignore the possibility of seeing her. I was lucky enough to see her on that day. I didn't take the same metro to the city. But at the Rajiv Chowk metro station, I heard something I was dying to hear for years. The heard the loveliest voice of my life.

Present Day

PARI

I shut the book and rushed to the bathroom. I thought, "What is happening to me? Why have I become so vulnerable?" I could feel the deepest pain in my heart. I didn't know whether I should scold him for his stupidities or should I hate him for chasing a girl or should I appreciate him for his stupid efforts to see his love. I was so puzzled. I didn't know for how long I had stayed in the bathroom, but those moments were some of the toughest moments of my life. A part of me was eager to read the last few pages of Aarush's diary and another part of me was afraid of treading upon something I didn't want to acknowledge. Some unknown detail of his life. I booked a cab, absolutely unsure of what I was doing. Maybe I was scared of something which was anything but scary. Maybe I was trying to escape from something that was inevitable. I just felt like escaping once more. But I couldn't. Everyone is not lucky enough to have second chances. And escaping has never been the right choice. I was panting, but I had to face Aarush. I couldn't escape anymore.

PARI

I always wanted to follow my dreams, being an independent and strong girl. I was perfectly on track. After University, I moved to the capital and God has been kind to me. I got a job with a company that paid for my travels. I went on a roller coaster ride. I was touching the sky in no time. I thought chasing my dream was more important, but I started missing my best buddy, Aarush. I soon realized that I had left behind something precious. Yes, I should have said goodbye. But it was difficult. Many times, this name has been both disturbing and charming, all at once. I could pass hours just thinking about him. But I couldn't gather the courage to call him. I believed we were not meant to go beyond the realms of friendship. So, I didn't want to put restrictions on his way of life. I could only envy his way of living, just spreading happiness all around. His presence lights up the environment. It was very difficult not to fall for him. I never intentionally wanted to be in that situation, but it just happened. Now I had to confess before things go out of hand. I have met so many people around the world. I have guided many people to discover beautiful places and have inspired so many people to travel. I often tell my readers or my clients, "Every moment of life, every place can be made beautiful. We just need beautiful eyes to look at it, and the right company by our side. We can't have everything at the same time. We can't be everywhere. So it's better if we try to enjoy the things we have". But

I always missed one special person. I would have been more than happy to see the world with him. I wish I could dial his number and tell him how I felt. But, I was scared. I never want him to suffer because of me. Unexplainable reasons always kept us away from the things our heart badly wanted. I kept on dumping my memories, trying to forget the past. But I wanted to go back to him. I wanted to confess. I was waiting for some miracle to happen. I hope he will forgive me. Yes, a good friend always does.

And it just happened. I couldn't resist myself from calling him when I saw him at the metro station. I couldn't believe my eyes. I could feel my heartbeat. Yes, it was real. I could see Aarush a few meters away. I didn't want to know where he was for the last four years, what he was doing in those years. I just wanted to see him, be with him. I wanted to smile with him. It was impulsive, and I was happy that it was impulsive. At least my rational self couldn't stop me from calling out, "AARUSH."

AARUSH

We had already finished two rounds of coffee and I was busy playing candy crush. Pari took a long break, and finally, she appeared. I was used to playing candy crush when I felt nervous. Yes, I was nervous indeed. After she settled in her seat, I asked Pari "Are you ok?"

She was shaken. It was clear that a lot of things were going on in her mind. I wanted to know everything.

"Did you like it?", I asked.

"Yes, but the story is incomplete", Pari said.

"How can you say that?", I said.

"It doesn't say anything about Tia and Aarush. Where they vanished, what Aarush did. And most importantly, if it is not happy then it is not the end", Pari said.

"But it's not always possible to end on a happy note. That's why words like 'sacrifices', 'forgiveness' and 'surrender' exist", I said. Pari did not seem convinced with my answer. Maybe she was looking for something else. Something positive, but I was tired of being positive. I had lost the charm in my personality.

"But one last page is yet to be completed", I continued.

"Are you angry with her decision when she left you?", Pari asked

"I don't think I was angry, but I was sad. I felt helpless when I couldn't contact her. I felt bad because I couldn't take any initiative to keep the friendship going after all we were best friends. But I was sure she must have her reasons. And I was always happy for her. But you know we can never be selfless, so I always waited for her. I checked my mobile every morning excepting a new massage, but it never flashed".

"Did you ever try to talk to Tia?", Pari was curious.

"I don't know how to answer it, or what to say. Initially yes, I tried, I tried to contact her. But it never worked out. She was chasing her career. I felt I was no longer important to her. I always kept myself updated with her tour updates, her travelogue. She had travelled a lot: Paris, Austria, Pisa. She was everywhere. At times, I have waited in front of her office, just for one look. Pillar no. 178 by her lane was the only witness to how eagerly I waited for her. She has walked past me without noticing me. And I have tried to satisfy my heart by catching those fleeting glances. Sometimes, I felt like a man with a very low moral stature. Stalking girls. But, I also felt my love for her was pure. I often cursed myself for not being true to myself, for not being able to tell her my feelings. The first few months, to be specific the first year, without her was quite unbearable. I realized how dependent I was. I was just left with the love I felt for her. And with time I felt at ease, no more pain. I decided that I would love her, no matter wherever she stays or what she thinks". I stopped for a while after saying this as the pain in my heart became impossible to bear. Just the thought of losing someone so dear to me. I looked away from Pari. Sometimes, it's important to just speak your heart out to someone. Someone whom you can trust, and someone who will never judge you.

"Why didn't you stop her?", Pari asked.

"I don't know. I never wanted to know. Sometimes, I feel I should have or could have, but I respect her decision. When we love someone, we try to respect their decision and gracefully try to accept the consequences. And I had no right to stop her. She was chasing her dream. I have always encouraged her to chase her dreams and couldn't selfishly and hold her back", I sighed.

"Why don't you ask her why she left you?", Pari asked.

"Perhaps I know her reasons. It was a difficult choice and I respect that she was brave enough to make a choice when I was just expecting for things to work out. Maybe she was planning something for both of us. So, it was always complicated and I thought it was better not to influence her decision by infusing my thoughts. We should do what the heart wants because it is the heart that bears the pain when logic fails. Most importantly, I believe that love never dies, whether you express it or not. It remains and its beautiful. It is beautiful to live in the hope that one day your love will come back to you. It is beautiful to remember your love without caring about reciprocation. Love constructs a platform where there is no place for sadness, no place for jealousy", I said.

"So, do you love her?", Pari asked after a long pause.

It was one of the toughest yet cutest questions I had ever faced, but I couldn't find the exact reason why. I didn't know if I was over thinking or I was actually stupid. I braved the question with a smile. I was ready for the consequences. I was not afraid of losing because friends always forgive.

"The last page is yet to be complete. Will you please...?", I stammered.

THE DIARY: Last Page

If you are reading this, that means you know a lot. Perhaps everything. Hope you do not get me wrong. I apologize if I have hurt you. Sometimes, we realize the importance of a person only after they leave. But, I always knew you are important to me. Actually, I never imagined a time like this would come. That day, when you called me at the metro station, I started thinking of new possibilities. I won't force anyone to be with me, but I couldn't go away from you. I feel guilty and regret my silence. I regret that I failed to be the friend you wanted to keep for life. I just know that if I get my love back, I won't allow any misunderstandings to create a distance between us. If time gives me an opportunity to hug my love, I won't loosen my grip. If I am allowed to hold her hand, I won't leave it. I am trying to live the life you had envisioned. I had gone to Mussoorie from where I saw the mighty Himalayas. How big it is! Yes, it was always good to see new places. You were so right. Then I went to Agra, "Wah Taj". I was mesmerized by the beauty of Taj. I witnessed the wonder of love. Everyone was enjoying the symbol of love, irrespective of caste, colour and religion. I went to Rishikesh. It was thrilling. I have realized how wrong I was in saying, "we can't be everywhere. So it's better we try to enjoy the things we have". How stupid I was. The world has so much more to offer. There is so much to be explored and so much to be enjoyed. I realized that we need to widen our horizons and try to reach and explore as many places as we can rather than being complacent and sticking to our comfort zone. I went to the temple to pray, went to the church to confess, went to the mausoleum to find peace, but it was not there. If it were to be found there so easily, God wouldn't have been so cruel to keep it away from us. I have travelled to many other places in India, but I have always missed someone. Maybe my peace was always with the person I missed. For whom my heart was beating, who could hold my hands and guide me. Then one day, I heard a familiar voice call my name in Delhi. I was overwhelmed. It was the same voice I was dying to hear. I can't live the life you live but I can accompany you throughout your journey. I am still the person you used to know four years ago. The friend who made you laugh. I hope things have not changed much or if they have, then I hope they have changed for the better. I hope we can get a second chance.

It doesn't matter what I call you, Pari or Tia. Yes, I missed you. And I love you. I know our families don't share the same religion, but no religion is against love. I know why you left me years ago, but escaping is not always the solution. See how we have met again. Maybe it's in our destiny. I don't know where our love will lead us, but Miss Pariza Khan, "I love you! It's time I accepted it". If you can reciprocate my love, then I would cherish you forever.

CONCLUSION:

It was the most beautiful day of my life. Finally, the wait was over. I could say what I felt to the girl I have loved for years. Sometimes, we need to speak out. This choice I would say is a perfect one. And I was lucky that I was able to get back the love of my life. "Destiny" is a word or a mystery. Every now and then, when the situation goes out of control, we call it destiny. Maybe we were destined to meet again. A person's entire world can change in seconds. A special second can change his or her destiny. After all, God is the planner. When we come face to face with God's plan, we often stop thinking and then we either start accepting or fighting the situation. We call it our "destiny". We all are destined to follow a predefined path, but what if God allows us to create own destiny? What if he kept it blank to be recreated by us? Then, we can just assume why something happens. Why people change their perception? Why we escape and so on. These kinds of question do not come with satisfactory answers. Still, we try to find the answers. Still, we fight to make things work out and still, we believe that we can turn an adverse situation to our favour. Perhaps this belief is what we refer to as "Hope". Hope is purely what we plan for life or expect from life and destiny is what He has planned for us. And one fine day, life says it's over. No more hope or destiny to bother about! Everyone may not be lucky enough to have the second chance. Yes, I am a lucky guy. And finally, the wait is over.

About the Author

Nikhil is a banking professional, working with a public sector bank. He got his MBA degree in marketing from Tezpur Central University, Assam. He spent his childhood in the serene island of Majuli, surrounded by river Brahmaputra. "Over a Cup of Coffee" is his first book. He loves writing, trying to bring real emotions and feelings into his writings. His other passions include watching football, as well as being an avid traveler. He presently lives in Greater Noida.